BEANObooks

published under licence by

MINX IDOL

It was the time of the week Minnie's teachers most dreaded. The P.E teachers were wearing shin pads. The drama teachers were carrying shields from the last production of King Arthur. The headmaster was wearing a crash helmet under his mortarboard.

It was time for school assembly.

The headmaster looked out over the sea of writing children and groaned. Then he took a deep breath, put a megaphone to his mouth and let out a bellow.

"QUIET!!!"

The smallest children in the front row were blown backwards by the force of the yell, but it quietened the pupils down just enough.

"I have an important announcement to make," roared the headmaster hoarsely. "Then you can all clear off back to your classrooms!"

"Get on with it!" called a voice from class 3B.

"Look behind you!" added a voice from 4A.

"This is not a panto!" bawled the headmaster. His mortarboard slipped to one side. "The school governors, in their wisdom, have decided to hold a music talent competition."

There was a loud cheer and he glared around the assembly hall.

"Why they think they'll find talent here is a mystery to me!" he growled. "But they have decided that the winner will sing at the end-of-year show, after all the usual class plays."

The maths teacher broke into a cold sweat at the very thought of it.

The woodwork teacher fanned himself with a sheaf of school reports.

"Moving on,"

roared the headmaster, "we have had another complaint about a pupil from this school. A pupil who was wearing red and black…"

All eyes swivelled to where Minnie and Dennis were sitting. Minnie glared back at them. (Dennis was too busy flicking gobstoppers at Walter the Softy to pay much attention.)

"… and wearing a beret," finished the headmaster. Minnie scowled and prepared to deny everything.

After the assembly, the pupils charged out of the hall, trying not to get jammed in the doorway.

"How wonderful!" lisped Soppy Susan. "I will sing a sweet and beautiful song, I'm sure to win!"

"I'll sing a song about food!" said Fatty Fudge.

"It all sounds totally stupid," said Minnie. "Singing on stage is for soppy softies!"

"Oh yeah?" grinned Dennis as he elbowed Walter out of the way. "Just as well you won't be singing, Minx, or we'd all be deaf!"

"Humph!" said Minnie. "At least I'd be better than you!"

"It's not stupid," added Soppy Susan pompously. "My Daddy told me all about it last night – he's on the board of governors you know – and he said that this isn't just about the end-of-year show."

"What do you mean?" asked Fatty, while Minnie crossed her eyes.

"There's a famous music producer visiting school shows for a new TV programme," said Soppy Susan. "They're searching for fresh new talent and they're going to invite all the best acts to appear on TV!"

"TV!" gasped Fatty. "You mean... I could be famous?"

"Well," simpered Soppy Susan, "I think you'll find I'm the most likely person to win the competition."

For once Minnie didn't offer a cheeky remark to keep Susan in her place. Instead, she was having a daydream. There she stood, on the stage, surrounded by people cheering and bowing to her. Music producers fought to offer her recording contracts. People travelled hundreds of miles to hear her sing.

"All that lovely dosh!" Minnie thought. "I'd never be skint again!"

She started to think that entering the talent competition wasn't such a bad idea after all! There was just one teeny tiny snag.

Minnie couldn't sing.

First she practised in the house. But her voice kept shattering glass.

"Out!" Mum ordered, clamping her hand over Minnie's mouth. "If you shatter any more glasses we won't have anything to drink from!"

Next she practised in the park. But every time she began to sing, the birds started dropping from the trees in shock.

"Clear orf!" bellowed the park warden. "Leave my birds alone, you little minx, and stop that 'orrible noise!"

Then Minnie tried practising in the changing rooms of the public swimming pool. Her voice echoed and bounced off the tiles. In the pool, babies screamed, grown men wept and one little old lady had to be rescued by the lifeguard.

10

"OUT!" roared the lifeguard, as soon as he had clambered out of the deep end. Minnie scarpered and walked home.

"Humph, people don't know good music when they hear it!" she grumbled. "My voice is great for minxing, but maybe I should try something else for the competition…"

Twenty minutes later, Minnie scrambled down from the loft, covered in dust and clutching Dad's old guitar.

"If I can't be a singer, I'll win the talent competition as a musician!" she chortled. She plugged the guitar in to the amp and ran her plectrum across the strings.

11

SCREEOOWWWAAHHHOOHHHEEEEECCHHHH!

The windows rattled and, down in the kitchen, Mum fell to the floor in a hail of saucepans. Chester the cat shot straight into the air like a rocket and landed on Dad's head with all his claws out.

"YOWEEEE!" hollered Dad, running around the sitting room and trying to shake Chester off.

"MEOOOWWEEEK!" spat Chester, as Minnie tried out a chord on the guitar and the house reverberated.

"Hmm, I think I'll try a song," said Minnie. As she launched into the first few bars, there was chaos for a mile around the house. Pets dived for cover as the hideous high-pitched sounds reached their ears.

The grass in the gardens wilted and tried to get back underground. The police switchboard was jammed with calls from people complaining about noise pollution.

Minnie finished her first song and turned up the volume another few notches. More and more electricity was diverted to her amp as the power increased. Lights started to fail all over Beanotown. Traffic lights stopped working and there was a massive traffic jam in the centre of town. Minnie turned up the power a little more. Fuses blew and light bulbs shattered. Then she cranked up the power to its highest setting. It was more than the power grid could take! Over at the power station, the main grid started to smoke and flash.

"There's a massive power drain!" hollered the head engineer.

Then, with a loud **WHUMP!**, the grid exploded!

Over at Minnie's house, the guitar suddenly lost its volume. Minnie frowned at it.

"Maybe being a guitarist wasn't such a good idea after all," she muttered. "I know! I'll go and check out what the competition is up to!"

The following day, Minnie raced to Soppy Susan's house and peered over the garden fence. Soppy Susan was standing in the middle of the garden with two of her soppiest friends.

"Now, is everybody ready?" asked Susan. "Let's take it from the top! And remember, we're the best and we're going to win!"

Minnie's eyes narrowed. Then Soppy Susan started to sing a sweet, sickly lullaby. The two other girls joined in, doing the harmonies.

"Yuck!" groaned Minnie. "That's the soppiest song I've ever heard!"

But she had to admit that they were holding the tune. No birds were dropping out of the trees. No glasses were shattering.

"Humph," Minnie said. "If I can't sing and I can't play a guitar, there's only one thing I can do.

SABOTAGE!"

On the day of the talent competition, all the performers lined up in the wings of the school stage. Soppy Susan's band was first in the queue. They were all clutching bottles of water and doing feeble vocal exercises.

"We have to look after our voices," simpered Susan, rattling her tambourine. "When we're stars, we will have to treat our voices like musical instruments!"

"Not if I've got anything to do with it!" chortled Minnie, pulling a pepper pot from under her beret. While the band wasn't looking, she poured pepper into their bottles of water.

"Can we have the first act please?" called the judges. Soppy Susan and her band made their way out to the stage, swigging down their water. But just as the music began to play, they turned bright pink in the face. Their eyes streamed and they started to cough.

"Is this your act?" asked one of the judges. "Not very musical, is it? You sound like croaking frogs! No thank you!"

Susan and her band were led off the stage, sobbing and coughing at the same time.

"One down," chuckled Minnie, rubbing her hands together. She headed off to find Fatty Fudge.

Fatty was busy testing how many cupcakes he could fit into his mouth at once. His trumpet was leaning against his chair. Minnie crept up behind him and pulled a small tin of extra-sticky treacle from her pocket. While he wasn't looking, Minnie smeared the treacle on his cupcakes and waited. Fatty's fingers stretched out and he took a cupcake in each hand. But as he tried to transfer them to his mouth, he realised that something was wrong. He couldn't let go! The cupcakes were glued to his hands!

"Help! Help!" cried Fatty, waving the cakes around and trying to shake them off.

"You can't play the trumpet like that, boy!" roared the headmaster.

"Never mind the trumpet, my cupcakes are ruined!" wailed Fatty.

Minnie chortled and headed off to find Dennis.

Minnie had a very busy afternoon. Each time the judges called for the next act, something went wrong.

Somebody hid Dennis's drum kit in the dressmaking shop, where they knew Dennis would never go.

Somebody told Pie Face that a bakery on the other side of town was giving away free pies. He disappeared in a cloud of dust.

Somebody filled Walter the Softy's recorder with marmalade. When he tried to play it, no sound came out. Walter blew very hard and SPLAT! He squirted marmalade into the head judge's eye.

"DISQUALIFIED!" roared the head judge in a fury. "NEXT!"

"Er, there's only one act left," said the headmaster.

"Well, thank goodness for that!" bellowed the head judge, wiping his eye with a hanky. "That act wins by default, so we can all go home!"

"You don't understand!" cried the headmaster in desperation. "The last act is… Minnie!"

"I don't care who she is. She's performing at the end-of-school show and that's final!" roared the head judge, who wanted to get home. "Now, get this marmalade off me!"

On the night of the show, the hall was packed. Parents squirmed on their seats, hoping their children wouldn't do anything too awful. Teachers mopped their brows and wished it was all over. At the back of the hall, the TV crew set up their equipment and the famous music producer got ready to listen.

One by one, each class presented

their plays. Class 1 did Robin Hood. Class 2 did King Arthur. Class 3 did George and the Dragon, which ended in tears when the back end of the dragon had an argument with the front end and split in two before George had a chance to fight it.

At last all the plays were over. Parents and teachers heaved a sigh of relief. Only Minnie's parents were still tense.

"And now," announced the headmaster, "the moment we've all been... ahem... looking forward to."

The music producer was nudged awake by the cameraman.

"Minnie will now delight you with her musical skill!" said the headmaster. Minnie leapt onto the stage with Dad's guitar and launched into her performance.

As the music rang around the hall, Mum and Dad opened their mouths in amazement. The headmaster pinched himself to check he wasn't dreaming. The music teacher staggered backwards and collapsed onto the Biology teacher.

Minnie was good!

She was better than good. She was amazing!

The audience was dancing in the aisles! The TV crew was going wild with excitement! The music producer was shouting something about a recording contract. Even the headmaster was clapping along.

But suddenly the headmaster noticed something. There was a power cord trailing across the back of the stage and into the wings. The headmaster walked backstage and peered into the wings. The power cord led behind a swathe of curtain and behind the curtain was a little CD player… blasting out the song that Minnie was playing. She had faked the whole thing!

There was a strange squeal from Minnie's fake guitar as the headmaster pulled the plug out of the wall.

"Uh-oh!" said Minnie, as the headmaster strode towards her. "Time to scarper!"

But it was too late. The headmaster gripped the back of her jumper and stopped her in her tracks.

"Oh no you don't, you little minx!" he bellowed. "Thought you could fool us all, did you? You're not going to get away with this!"

"Hold it! Hold it!" yelled the TV director. He was grinning from ear to ear. "That was fantastic television!" he burbled. "That will hook millions! My viewing figures will rocket! Minnie, you're wonderful!"

"Wh... what?" gasped the headmaster.

"I think I need to get my hearing tested," Dad whispered to Mum.

"Is this some kind of joke?" asked the headmaster furiously.

"No, not at all!" smiled the TV director. "I'm sick of filming good children! I want to make Minnie famous – as the biggest minx in the country!"

The headmaster's mouth fell open and he let go of Minnie, who straightened her beret and walked to the front of the stage.

"The biggest minx in the country?" she said, as a huge grin spread across her face. "Now that is music to my ears!"

CATWALK COMMOTION

"No way!" Minnie yelled.

The windows rattled and the walls shook. Chester scooted for cover under the sofa.

"Not if I live to be a hundred!" bellowed Minnie. "Not if you torture me and lock me in a dungeon! Never!"

"You'll do it whether you like it or not!" Mum said through gritted teeth. "Tell her, Dad!"

"Leave me out of this!" trembled Dad, hiding behind his newspaper. "What do I know about fashion?"

"Minnie, I'm warning you…" Mum said, putting her hands on her hips.

"Oh yeah?" Minnie grumbled. "Or what? You can't make me do it!"

Mum had spent weeks planning and organising a grand fashion show for her favourite charity, Help the Gormless. The show was that evening, and all the tickets had been sold. But, at the last minute, Mum had realised that she hadn't hired enough models.

"All the children from the neighbourhood are going to help me out," Mum told Minnie. "Susan is going to be there, and Walter…"

"Soppy Susan and Walter the Softy?" bellowed Minnie. "Is that supposed to make me want to help? Why don't you get Dad to do some modelling?"

"Hmm, not a bad idea," said Mum thoughtfully. Dad shot into

the air as if he had been sitting on a drawing pin.

"Er... um... just remembered, very busy, must mow the hedge and prune the lawn, see you later..."

He scurried out and Mum looked at Minnie again.

"Even Fatty Fudge is going to give us a hand!" she said with a bright smile. "How do you think you'll feel when you're the only one not up on that catwalk?"

"Relieved," said Minnie, darkly.

"It would be so wonderful to see you wearing something really pretty for a change," sighed Mum, clasping her hands together. "I'd love to see you in a sweet little pink hat with a white frill instead of that horrid beret."

Minnie clenched her fists and stuck out her lower lip.

"My beret isn't meant to look good!" she roared.

"That's an understatement," Mum smirked.

"My beret is where I keep all my most minxing weapons, and there is no way I'm gonna replace it with a pink lacy hat!"

"It's only for a few hours!" Mum pleaded.

"Not even for a few seconds!" shouted Minnie.

Mum breathed in and counted to ten. Then she cracked her knuckles, folded her arms and fixed Minnie with a fierce glare.

"I didn't want to have to do this," she said. "But you leave me no choice. I've ordered and I've pleaded with you. I've told you and I've asked you nicely. Now there's only one thing left I can do."

Minnie backed away. She went pale. "Not... not..."

"Yes!" exclaimed Mum. "I've taken your Beano collection hostage! If you don't get up there on that catwalk and take part in my Help the Gormless fashion show, I'll line the hamster's cage with your comics!"

"You fiend!" howled Minnie. "I've got the best comic collection in Beanotown! You can't line the hamster's cage with the best comic ever!"

"I can and I will," said Mum.

"I feel faint!" Minnie gasped, dropping onto the sofa and fanning herself with Dad's paper.

"All you have to do is put on a beautiful dress and look like a princess for the evening," wheedled Mum.

"It's totally stupid and dead embarrassing," Minnie sighed. "But it looks as though I'm gonna have to go through with it. Either I dress like an idiot... or I lose my precious collection!"

"I knew you'd see sense!" Mum cackled, rubbing her hands together. "You're coming with me right now to try your outfit on."

Half an hour later, Minnie was standing in front of a long mirror in the dressing room at the town hall, where the fashion show was going to be held.

"Pass me a bucket," she groaned. "I think I'm gonna throw up!"

"You're a vision!" cried Mum in delight. "I never thought I'd see the day – my little Minnie in a dress!"

The dress was long and made of pink satin. White bows were stitched on all over the material and the hems were edged with thick purple lace. As Minnie stared at herself in horror, Mum put a cerise velvet sash around her waist and tied it in a big bow at the back.

37

"I'm finished," said Minnie in shock. "The minute I'm seen in this, no one will ever take me seriously again! My minxing days are over."

"Don't be silly, dear," Mum fussed, trying to pull Minnie's beret off her head. Minnie grasped hold of it with both hands.

"No way!" she said. "You can't take that too!"

Mum recognised the glint of stubbornness in Minnie's eyes and stopped pulling at the beret.

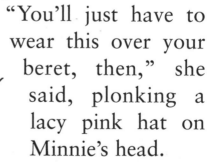

"You'll just have to wear this over your beret, then," she said, plonking a lacy pink hat on Minnie's head.

"Ugh," groaned Minnie, turning away from her

38

reflection. "This is an emergency! I've gotta think of something quick!"

"Start thinking about how you're going to look on the catwalk," said Mum brightly, as Minnie groaned again. "Now, all you need is a little touch of lipstick…"

"No!" bellowed Minnie. She pulled off the hat and struggled with the sash. "I won't do it! You can't make me!"

"You're right, I can't make you," said Mum calmly. "You can walk away any time you like… you just won't see your Beano collection again, that's all."

"This is blackmail!" Minnie complained.

"I've learned a thing or two from you, dear!" said Mum. "Now, take off the dress and pick that hat up off the floor. You'll be wearing it later!"

Mum turned away with a big grin on her face and Minnie frowned.

"I can't wear that dress," she muttered, "and I can't lose the coolest comic collection ever. There's only one thing for it...

"the dress has to go!"

There were only a few hours left before the show was due to start and Mum had brought the dress home to make a few tiny alterations to it. When she had finished, she hung it on the kitchen door and beamed at Minnie.

"You'll be the belle of the ball in that dress," she said. "People will be talking about you all over Beanotown."

"Yeah," said Minnie under her breath, "but not because of that dress, if I have anything to do with it!"

Minnie waited while Mum bustled around the kitchen. It wasn't going to be easy sneaking the dress away from Mum's protection. Suddenly she had an idea. She walked into the sitting room and twitched the curtains. Mum's ears pricked up. Her gossip radar had been triggered.

"Ooooooh!" said Minnie in a loud voice. "You'll never believe what Mrs-across-the-road is doing now!"

There was a zooming sound and Mum was next to the sitting room window, panting.

"Where? What?" she asked. But Minnie wasn't there. She whizzed back into the kitchen, grabbed the dress and charged out to the garden, where Dad was planting vegetables. Minnie bundled the dress into a ball and shoved it into one of the holes Dad had dug.

"I'm not getting involved, I know nothing," Dad murmured to himself as the pink satin disappeared under the soil. Minnie jumped to her feet and strolled back into the kitchen, whistling.

"WHERE'S THAT DRESS?"

Mum bellowed. "And what was Mrs-across-the-road doing?"

But before Minnie could think of an answer, Chester the family cat walked into the kitchen, dragging something large... and muddy... and pink.

"The dress!" squealed Mum. "Oh well done, Chester! There's still time to wash it!"

She bundled the dress into the washing machine and Minnie glared at Chester.

"Just you wait," she muttered as he washed his whiskers smugly. "I'm not beaten yet!"

When the dress was hanging out on the line, Minnie sneaked into the garden with one of Dad's old fountain pens.

"Let's see you survive this!" she hissed, squirting blue ink all over the front of the dress.

"Ha! If there's no dress, there's no embarrassment for me and I get to keep my comics!"

But when Mum saw the stain, she just shrugged her shoulders.

44

"Oh dear," she said. "What a shame, Minnie grinned. "Looks like I can't be part of the fashion show after all."

"Oh don't be silly, dear," Mum laughed. "I had this dress made especially for you! So of course it's made of totally washable and wipe-clean material!"

She wiped the ink with a damp cloth and it all came off. Minnie clapped her hand to her forehead.

"Indestructible fashion!" she groaned as Mum walked away to put the dress somewhere safe.

Minnie went out to get some target practice and try to think of another plan. As she scored a direct hit on Dennis's backside with a rotten tomato, she had a brainwave.

"Aha!" she shouted, loading up her catapult again. "I've got it! If I can't destroy the dress, I'm just gonna have to put a stop to the fashion show!"

 Minnie spent most of the afternoon trying to sabotage the fashion show. She sneaked into the dressing room and stirred itching powder into the face cream.

She stuffed cotton wool into the sound equipment.

She hid all the lighting engineer's bulbs.

And she put a big notice on the door of the town hall saying:

CLOSed foR REpAirs
ABSoLutely No fashioN Shows HEre TODAy
(you miGHt as weLL GO HomE!)

But it was no use.

All the models brought their own face cream.

The sound engineer decided that he liked the muffled sound and left the cotton wool where it was.

GYM KIT

The lighting engineer had a spare set of bulbs.

And Mum found the notice on the door and tore it down before anyone could see it.

"You can't do anything about it!" she told Minnie. "The show must go on! Oh, how I love show business! The makeup! The costumes! The glamour!"

"Loopy," growled Minnie as she was pushed into the dressing room. "Completely loopy."

Minnie's moment had almost arrived. The audience was waiting, the music was playing and Fatty Fudge was just walking off the catwalk. His outfit was a summer holiday look, complete with chocolate ice cream.

As he stepped down from the

catwalk, Minnie squirted a splodge of extra-slippy makeup right under Fatty's great big feet. He skidded on it, waved his arms wildly and fell into Soppy Susan. His ice cream smeared all over her dress!

"My beautiful frock!" wailed Soppy Susan, tears squirting from her eyes. "How am I ever going to be a model now?"

"Don't worry!" said Minnie, thinking fast. She was wearing her own clothes underneath her outfit, so she pulled off the hideous pink dress and handed it to Susan. "Here, you can wear this instead!"

"It's **GORGEOUS!**" squealed Soppy Susan, pulling on the dress and ramming the hat onto her head. Then Minnie heard her name being announced. She tore up the steps and marched down the catwalk.

"And next we have Minnie," announced the presenter in a smooth voice. "Minnie is wearing – oh my good lord!"

The presenter did a double take as Minnie paused at the end of the catwalk and gave a twirl. Then he realised he would have to improvise.

"Er, Minnie is wearing... a striking black-and-red ensemble with matching... er... worn-look boots. Her hat is a... er... black beret in the Parisian style—" Minnie swept a catapult from beneath her beret, "—with matching... um... accessories."

Minnie looked down at Mum, who was sitting in the front row, and gave her a huge wink. Then she turned and marched back up the catwalk, much to the presenter's relief.

When Minnie walked back into the dressing room at the end of the show, Mum was waiting for her. She looked ready to burst.

"You... you... minx!" Mum exploded. "Your Beano collection is a thing of the past! It's going to line the hamster's cage as soon as I get home!"

"Hang on a minute," grinned Minnie. "You said that I had to get up on the catwalk and take part in the fashion show! Well – I did that! So you can't take my comics!"

"You just wait and see!" roared Mum. "I'm not—"

She was interrupted by a loud bang as the door of the dressing room burst open and a huge crowd of people swarmed in, all talking nineteen to the dozen and snapping photos of Minnie.

"Girl power is the new black!"

"Eh?" said Minnie.

"You've got the latest look, darling!" screamed one woman. "We're all famous fashion editors—"

"Some of us are more famous than others, darling!" snapped another woman, pushing the first out of the way. "We adore your style, Minnie, we're think you're absolutely IT!"

"You're completely different!" gushed a man in a purple bow tie.

"She's different all right," Mum grumbled.

"You're going to be on the covers of all the next issues!" said the first woman. "We want lots and lots of pictures of your fabulous new look!"

"Hmm, does that mean you'll pay me lots and lots of dosh?" Minnie asked.

"Of course, darling!" cried the second woman. "By the time these pictures come out, every girl in the country will want to look just like you!"

"Excellent!" Minnie grinned. "Hear that, Mum? I'm gonna have enough dosh to buy loads more comics and annuals – and I think I'll get the hamster a present too! How about a miniature Minnie outfit?"

But there was no reply. Mum had fainted dead away!

MINX OF THE MATCH

The rain spattered against the windowpane and Minnie sighed again.

"**I'm BORED!**" she bellowed.

"When I was a lad, we used to have to entertain ourselves," began Dad.

Everyone knew what that meant – Dad was going to start talking about the good old days. Chester the cat put his head under a cushion. Minnie rolled her eyes. Mum muttered something about finishing the washing up and hurried out of the room.

"We used to have competitions between the raindrops rolling down the windowpane and think ourselves lucky!" Dad went on. Minnie's hand started to move towards her catapult.

"Ah, those were the days," he sighed happily.

"What, watching raindrops?" asked Minnie scornfully. "Sounds brilliant, Dad. Didn't you ever do anything exciting?"

"Exciting? Exciting?" cried Dad, bouncing up in his armchair. "I used to be a campaigner, you know, in my youth! Ah, the demonstrations! The smell of the paint as we made banners to wave! We made real nuisances of ourselves!"

Minnie's ears pricked up at the word 'nuisances'.

"Sounds like fun," she said thoughtfully.

"Oh, we had some great times," Dad chuckled. "It felt great to win a campaign – it even felt great running away when we got into trouble!"

A glint came into Minnie's eyes. It sounded as if campaigning could be a lot like minxing. All she needed was a cause to campaign for.

Minnie's chance came the very next day at school. After Mr Osborne had called the register, he gave a loud roar to silence the class and scowled at everyone.

"I have an announcement to make to the boys," he said.

"PAY ATTENTION AT THE BACK!"

Curly and Pie Face, who had been plotting something, jumped and looked up.

"Mr Pump has informed me that try-outs for the football team are going to be held tomorrow," Mr Osborne went on. "As you know, we need some good strong players on our team this year if we're going to stand a chance of winning the cup. So I want to see all you lads out there tomorrow, ready to try for the team. Got it?"

Up until that moment, Minnie hadn't been paying much attention. But then one of the more sporty girls in the class stuck her hand in the air.

"Sir, how come you're not asking the girls? And how come there are no girls on the team?"

"Er, ahem, harrumph!" said Mr Osborne, trying to think quickly.

"Never you mind that, young lady. You've got enough games you can play – you've got tennis and hockey and netball. Leave the football to the boys, there's a good girl."

"Yeah, football's a boys' game!" jeered Curly.

"Stick with the easy games!" Pie Face laughed.

"Girls can't play football!" scoffed Fatty Fudge.

Minnie whipped her catapult from beneath her beret and fired a small but powerful water bomb at Fatty Fudge, who let out a loud wail.

"That's rubbish!" Minnie announced. "I bet any girl in this classroom could beat you at football, Fatty Fudge! I'm gonna start a campaign and make the teachers let all the girls play football!"

"Hurray!" cheered the sporty girls.

"Oh no," groaned Soppy Susan. "Can I do sewing class instead?"

"Nonsense, Minnie!" bellowed Mr Osborne. "We can't have the girls playing football! It's not done!"

"I won't stop campaigning until we're all allowed to try out for the team!" Minnie roared, jumping onto her desk and waving her beret in the air. "And every girl in the class is gonna help out!"

"It's not fair!" wailed one of Soppy Susan's friends. "Please, sir, we don't want—"

But she was silenced by a well-aimed blast from Minnie's peashooter.

Soppy Susan and her friends started to cry, but their sobs were drowned out by loud cheers from the sporty girls, and the sound of scared gulps from the boys.

"I'm not playing football with a bunch of girls!" Curly hollered.

"Scared we'll beat you?" Minnie asked, firing a small wad of paper up his nose with her peashooter.

"I don't want to get all muddy and cold and wet!" Soppy Susan shuddered.

"Football is for everyone!" Minnie shouted above the hubbub.

"I don't mind giving up football to the girls!" Walter the Softy told Spotty Perkins. "I'd rather do sewing anyway."

"Football for girls!
"Football for girls!
chanted the sporty girls, while Minnie kept time by banging her ruler on Fatty's head.

"Don't make me play!" sobbed Matilda. "I've got a weak chest! I don't feel well! I want my mumsy!"

"SILENCE!" roared Mr Osborne helplessly. "QUIET! Minnie, there is no way we're going to let the girls try out for the team, and that's final!"

He scurried out of the room and headed for the safety of the staff room. He told the P.E. teacher, Mr Pump, all about what had happened.

"Ho ho ho!" rumbled Mr Pump, sticking out his chest and looking very fit and healthy. "Football isn't a game for girls! They're far too rough!"

Mr Osborne snuggled into an armchair with the staff biscuit tin.

"I don't want to think about it any more," he said. Then his ears pricked up.

"Did you h-hear something?" he trembled.

"Sounded like Minnie's voice," said the headmaster, who was chewing on some headache pills in the corner. "Quick, there's still a chance to escape!"

Mr Pump peered out through the

barred staff room window.

"She's marching up and down with a banner!" he exclaimed. "It's got a picture on it – a picture of a girl holding a football! She's shouting something too... ARGGGHH!"

Mr Pump dived to the staff room floor as a water bomb flew in through the window and narrowly missed him.

"YOWURGHH!"

yelled the headmaster as the water bomb exploded in his face.

"Football for girls! Football for girls!" chanted Minnie, firing a stink bomb with her catapult. It flew through the staff-room window. Within seconds Mr Pump, Mr Osborne and the headmaster were all at the window, gasping in fresh air and looking rather green in the face.

"Mr Pump!" wheezed the headmaster. "I strongly suggest that you give in!"

"But the poor boys!" panted Mr Pump. "I'm trying to protect them! Who knows what will happen to them if they have girls on the team? They'll be wiped out!"

"It's a risk I'm willing to take!" said the headmaster, thinking of Dennis.

Mr Pump pulled out a large white handkerchief and waved it at Minnie.

"All right!" he called. "You win! The girls can try out for the team as well as the boys!"

"I knew they'd see sense," chortled Minnie.

The following morning, the whole of the class was lined up in front of the goal. The goalkeeper stood in front of it, grinning.

"Now listen up, you horrible lot!" roared Mr Pump. "We need three new players on the football team, so this is what we're going to do. Each pupil will try to score a goal. If you miss, you're out. The last three left in will be the three new players. Got it?"

"I don't like it!" wept Soppy Susan. "It's cold and I don't like my outfit!"

"It's not supposed to be fashionable," Minnie hissed. "You're first in line, so get up there and score a goal!"

Soppy Susan stood in front of the ball, her knobbly knees knocking together. She gave the ball a feeble little kick and screamed.

"My toe! OW! It hurts! Oh Mumsy!"

"NO!" roared Mr Pump.

It was Minnie's turn next. She jogged up to the ball and fired it into the back of the net so fast that it parted the goalkeeper's hair.

"GOAL!" roared Minnie.

One by one each pupil took a shot at the goal. Soon there were just four people left – Curly, Pie Face, Minnie and the sporty girl who had asked about football in the first place.

"The first one to miss is out!" said Mr Pump. Curly scored a goal, then Minnie hurtled another ball into the back of the net, while the goalkeeper cowered at the side.

"Easy shot," grinned Pie Face. But just as he was about to shoot, Minnie wafted a steaming, hot pie in front of his nose and he was so distracted that he ballooned his shot over the bar.

"The girls are in! Football is for girls!" Minnie cheered. "Two girls on the team! We're gonna beat everyone!"

"Yes," nodded Mr Pump. "You two are on the team along with Curly. Practice starts tomorrow – the cup match is just two weeks away!"

Two weeks later, Minnie stomped into the kitchen in her football kit and scowled at everyone. Chester quietly left the room.

"Ready for the cup match, Minnie," asked Mum.

"Humph," Minnie grumbled. "I'm fed up with football."

"But I thought you campaigned to be allowed onto the team?"

"I did," said Minnie.

"And I thought you and that other girl were the best players on the team?"

"We are," Minnie sighed.

"Then what's the problem?"

"We've had practice every day after school for two weeks." Minnie grumbled. "It's seriously cutting in to my minxing time! I'm gonna quit after the game today!"

"**Oh no!**" cried Mum (she had never known such a peaceful two weeks). "Don't do a thing like that!"

"Well, maybe I'll have to see what I think after the cup match," Minnie shrugged.

The first half of the match went very well. Minnie scored three goals and Mr Pump was overjoyed.

"Splendid idea of mine, letting girls onto the team," he told anyone who would listen. "The headmaster tried to stop me but I insisted!"

When the half-time whistle blew, the team went to have some refreshments.

"Good game," said Minnie, chomping on a large pie. "I reckon we're gonna win."

"Yeah, but I bet the prize will go to the other side," complained Curly.

"What are you talking about?" Minnie frowned. "What prize?"

"Didn't you know?" asked Curly. "Weren't you listening at practice yesterday?"

"I was too busy practising my

catapult skills to listen to old Pump," scoffed Minnie.

"There's gonna be a prize for the best player in the match," Curly explained. "They're giving away a day's exercise training with Beanotown Football Club! I bet their star players will give the winner a few tips as well."

Minnie's eyes opened wide. "Awesome prize," she said thoughtfully. "I could do with a prize like that. "

She looked across the field at the other team.

"I'm just gonna have to make sure I'm the star of the match," she murmured.

Two minutes into the second half, Minnie had already scored three more goals for her side and fouled three members of the other team.

Three minutes after that, she charged up the pitch, elbowed two midfielders out of the way and cannoned into the leftwinger, who went flying into the goal.

"You're supposed to score with the ball, not with the other team!" bellowed the referee.

Minutes later Minnie hurtled across the halfway line, slide tackled her own team's striker, sending turf and player flying, and sent him spinning like a top into the right back. They collapsed in a jumble of arms and legs.

The first aid team leader exchanged glances with his assistant.

"I think we're going to need some backup," he said.

The rest of the match was a whirl of bloodcurdling tackles, fouls, goals, more fouls and stretchers. Minnie kicked shins in the penalty area and clashed heads in midfield. By the end of the match, the score was 26-2 to Beanotown School (twenty more of Minnie's goals were disallowed) and there were just three members of the opposing team still standing.

All around the pitch, stretchers were being carried away and bandages were being applied. The headmaster was fanning himself with Minnie's school report. Mum and Dad were trying to leave without anyone recognising them.

The referee blew the final whistle and the players limped over to the table where the cup stood on a small table.

"I award this cup to Beanotown School," said the referee. "I'm sure we all – er – congratulate them..."

Curly took the cup and held it up high. There was a faint clap from one or two parents.

"And now for the grand prize," went on the referee. "This prize is awarded to the best player in the match. I have decided to award it to the captain of the losing team, for steering clear of Minnie and for avoiding serious injury. Well done! I hope you enjoy your day at the Beanotown Football Club!"

Everyone cheered as the boy shook hands with the referee. Everyone, that is, except Minnie. She marched up to the referee, one hand on her hip and the other poised to grab a weapon from her beret.

"I scored more goals than all the others put together!" she bellowed. "I should get the prize for best player!"

The referee checked his shin pads were in position and backed away behind a table.

"Now listen here, young – er – lady," he stammered. "It's not always about winning, you know. It's about being a good sport and not – er – cheating."

"Rubbish!" declared Minnie. "I've had enough of this stupid game! Everyone knows it's about how many goals you can score!"

She pulled out her catapult as the headmaster stepped in front of the referee.

"Minnie, wait a moment," he said. "You have won a prize too!"

"Really?" asked Minnie suspiciously. "What for?"

"Just come up here and I will tell you," said the headmaster with a tight smile.

Minnie took a step forward.

"Well?" she asked.

The headmaster picked up a megaphone. "All the players have spoken to me – from their stretchers!" he boomed. "They have voted to name Minnie 'Minx of the Match'!"

There was a stunned silence as Minnie gave a huge smile.

"Excellent title," she beamed, taking a step closer. "So what's my prize?"

"Well," smiled the headmaster, "I thought you might like to have some exercise training too."

"You mean I'm going to the Beanotown Football Club too?" Minnie grinned, stepping even closer to the headmaster.

"**NO!**" he roared, grabbing her by the collar and confiscating her weapons. "I mean you're going to get your exercise right here, helping to repair the pitch after all these slide tackles you made during the game!"

There was a rousing cheer and loud applause. Someone started singing

'One headmaster, there's only one Headmaster...'

"Huh, what a bummer!" scowled Minnie. "That's the last time I get involved in campaigning!"

OTHER FANTASTIC FICTION FROM

meadowside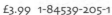
CHILDREN'S BOOKS

£3.99 1-84539-205-1

£3.99 1-84539-204-3

Join Dennis, the menacing
super-hero in three more
memorable menacing
stories featuring the
beano's bad boy!

Dennis and friends on
a school trip! Disaster
is definite in three
more stories of
menacing madness.

OTHER FANTASTIC FICTION FROM

meadowside
CHILDREN'S BOOKS

£3.99 1-84539-098-9

Follow the master of
menacing through a maze
of mischief and mayhem.

£3.99 1-84539-095-4

Grown-ups and softies
beware – Dennis is on
a mission to menace!

OTHER FANTASTIC FICTION FROM

meadowside
CHILDREN'S BOOKS

£3.99 1-84539-097-0

£3.99 1-84539-096-2

Everyone knows a menace
somewhere... Now read
about the greatest
menace ever!

Dennis is back!
Join the mighty menace
as he creates more
crazy chaos!

Written by RACHEL ELLIOT

Illustrated by BARRIE APPLEBY

published under licence by

185 Fleet Street, London, EC4A 2HS

www.meadowsidebooks.com

"The Beano"®©, "Minnie the Minx"®©
and associated characters
™©D.C. Thomson & Co., Ltd., 2006

Printed and bound in Great Britain by William Clowes Ltd, Beccles, Suffolk

10 9 8 7 6 5 4 3 2 1